Where Are You, Blue Kangaroo?

Emma Chichester Clark

Andersen Press
LONDON

for the one and only
Lily Brown

Copyright © 2000 by Emma Chichester Clark
The rights of Emma Chichester Clark to be identified as the author and illustrator
of this work have been asserted by her in accordance with the Copyright, Designs and Patents Act, 1988.
First published in Great Britain in 2000 by Andersen Press Ltd., 20 Vauxhall Bridge Road, London SW1V 2SA.
Published in Australia by Random House Australia Pty., 20 Alfred Street, Milsons Point, Sydney, NSW 2061.
All rights reserved. Colour separated in Switzerland by Photolitho AG, Zürich. Printed and bound in Italy
by Grafiche AZ, Verona.

10   9   8   7   6   5   4   3   2   1

British Library Cataloguing in Publication Data available.

ISBN 0 86264 923 4

This book has been printed on acid-free paper

Blue Kangaroo belonged to Lily.
He was her very own kangaroo.
Sometimes Blue Kangaroo disappeared and Lily would say,
"Where are you, Blue Kangaroo?"
And Blue Kangaroo waited for Lily to find him.

One day, Lily's friend, Florence, took Lily to the park.
"Hold tight to Blue Kangaroo," said Florence.

Lily swung on the swings, and she wasn't scared on the slide.

"I love ice-cream!" said Lily . . .

. . . and Blue Kangaroo
wondered if Lily
had forgotten him.

As they were leaving, Lily suddenly shrieked,
"Where are you, Blue Kangaroo?"
"Did you leave him on the slide?" asked Florence.

"Here he is!" smiled Lily.
"You must try to be more careful," said Florence.

The next Saturday, Lily's Aunt Jemima took Lily shopping.
"Hold tight to Blue Kangaroo," said Aunt Jemima.

On the bus, Lily met a nice lady wearing a large pink hat.

"I love buses," said Lily, as they reached
their stop . . .

. . . and Blue Kangaroo
wondered if he'd ever
see her again.

They hadn't gone very far, when Lily shrieked,
"Where are you, Blue Kangaroo?"

"You didn't leave him on the bus, did you, Lily?"
asked Aunt Jemima.

"I think you forgot someone!" said the nice lady in the
pink hat.
"Lily!" said Aunt Jemima. "You must be more careful."

On Sunday, Uncle George took Lily to the zoo.
"Hold tight to Blue Kangaroo," said Uncle George.

"I like lions . . ." said Lily,

". . . but I *love* monkeys. Can we buy them some nuts?"

And Blue Kangaroo
felt very anxious.

"Shall I get six bags?" asked Lily.
"No, just one . . ." said Uncle George,

". . . and then we'll visit the real kangaroos."
But Blue Kangaroo had gone already . . .

"WHERE ARE YOU,
BLUE KANGAROO?"
shrieked Lily.

"Is that your kangaroo?" asked the zoo-keeper.
"We'd better get him back before they get
too fond of him."

"You're lucky he didn't land up with the lions,"
said the zoo-keeper. "Now you tuck him away somewhere
safe."

That night Lily tucked Blue Kangaroo
up in bed. "We're going to the seaside
tomorrow . . ." she said, and she fell
asleep with Blue Kangaroo in her arms.

But Blue Kangaroo couldn't sleep.
He worried and worried.

Then he slipped out of bed, and hopped
across the carpet towards the door . . .

In the morning, Lily looked everywhere for Blue Kangaroo but she couldn't find him.

They looked in all the usual places.
"Did you leave him in the garden?" asked her mother.

Everyone searched high and low, but Blue Kangaroo was nowhere to be found.

"It looks as if you really have lost him this time,"
said Lily's mother.

Lily ran to her room and slammed the door.
"Where, oh *where* are you, Blue Kangaroo?" she sobbed.

Lily wiped her tears away . . . and guess who she saw?
"You naughty Blue Kangaroo!" she said . . .

. . . and she never let Blue Kangaroo
out of her sight,
ever, again.